This edition published 2009 by Geddes & Grosset,
David Dale House, New Lanark ML11 9DJ, Scotland
First published 1993, reprinted 1994, 1996, 2001, 2004, 2009

© 1993 Geddes & Grosset

ISBN 978 1 85534 571 3

Printed and bound in India

The Three Billy Goats Gruff

Retold by Judy Hamilton
Illustrated by R. James Binnie

Tarantula Books

There were once living in a field beside a river three billy goats. They were known as the Billy Goats Gruff and they were brothers, but they were not at all like each other. One was very big and fierce-looking with a big bushy beard and long curling horns. He was the oldest of the three. The middle-sized Billy Goat Gruff was not so big. He had a soft, wavy beard and shorter horns and looked more gentle! The youngest Billy Goat Gruff was very small and thin. He looked very timid. His horns were short and skimpy and he hardly had any beard at all.

The Billy Goats Gruff were happy together, munching away at the grass in the field.

However, three goats can munch an awful lot of grass, and after a while the grass in their field looked bare and thin. Soon it would all be gone.

Now, the Billy Goats Gruff could see that over the river was a bigger field, full of the longest, lushest, greenest grass that they had ever seen. For a long time they had wanted to cross the river to get to the other field, but there was a problem. The river was fast and deep, and the only way to get to the other side was over a rickety wooden bridge. Under the bridge there lived a fearsome ugly troll. Whenever anybody tried to cross the bridge, the troll would jump out of his hiding place and gobble them up. Nobody who knew about the troll dared to use the bridge.

The grass in the goats' field grew thinner and thinner. They were eating it faster than it could grow. The Billy Goats Gruff began to get thinner and thinner too. One day the eldest Billy Goat Gruff called his brothers to him.

"If we stay here much longer we will starve," he said. "We have no choice. We must try to cross the bridge. But how can we beat that ugly troll?"

The other two thought for a moment and then the youngest goat said, "I think I have a plan. Listen to me ..."

A few moments later, the youngest Billy Goat Gruff trotted bravely up to the bridge. He was to be the first to try to cross.

Taking a deep breath he stepped lightly onto the bridge. "Trip-trap, trip-trap, trip-trap" went his hooves on the rickety wood.

The troll jumped out, angry and ugly. "Who goes trip-trapping on my bridge?" he roared.

"Only the youngest Billy Goat Gruff," squeaked the little goat.

"Goody-goody, I'm going to gobble you up!" leered the troll.

"Wait a minute, Mr Troll," squeaked the youngest Billy Goat Gruff. "You can see how small and skinny I am. My big brother will be coming in a moment. He's much fatter, why spoil your appetite? Wait for him and gobble him up instead!"

The troll grumbled and groaned and thought for a moment, then spoke to the youngest Billy Goat Gruff.

"Very well, off you go! It sounds like your brother would make a much tastier meal. I shall wait for him and gobble him up!"

The youngest Billy Goat Gruff tripped and trapped over the bridge to the safety of the big green field on the other side of the river.

The troll climbed back down to his hiding place under the bridge to wait for the middle-sized Billy Goat Gruff to come along. A few moments later the middle-sized Billy Goat Gruff trotted bravely up to the bridge.

Taking a deep breath he stepped firmly onto the bridge. "TRIP-TRAP, TRIP-TRAP, TRIP-TRAP" went his hooves. The troll jumped out, angrier and uglier than before. "Who goes trip-trapping on my bridge?" he yelled.

"Only the middle-sized Billy Goat Gruff," replied the middle-sized goat, calmly.

"Goody-goody! I've been waiting for you! I'm going to gobble you up!" gloated the troll.

"Oh, no! I don't think that would be a good idea," said the middle-sized Billy Goat Gruff gently. "I know I'm bigger than the smallest goat, but my big brother, who is coming soon, is much bigger and fatter than I am. Why spoil your appetite? Wait for him and gobble him up instead!"

Once more the troll grumbled and groaned and thought for a moment.

"Oh, all right, off you go!" he grunted. "It sounds like your big brother would make an even tastier meal. I shall wait for him and gobble him up!"

The middle-sized Billy Goat Gruff tripped and trapped over the bridge to join his little brother in the safety of the big green field on the other side of the river. The troll climbed back down once again to his hiding place under the bridge to wait for the eldest Billy Goat Gruff to come along.

A few moments later the eldest Billy Goat Gruff trotted bravely up to the bridge.

Taking a deep breath, he stamped loudly onto the bridge. "TRIP-TRAP, TRIP-TRAP, TRIP-TRAP" went his hooves on the rickety wood.

The troll jumped out, angrier and uglier than ever. "Who goes trip-trapping on my bridge?" he bellowed.

"I am the eldest Billy Goat Gruff," announced the big goat proudly.

"Goody-goody! So YOU are the one I've been waiting for!" drooled the troll. "I'm going to gobble you up!"

"Oh no, Mr Troll, I don't think so!" The eldest Billy Goat Gruff tossed his horns in defiance.

The three Billy Goats Gruff never ran out of grass again. They tripped and trapped to and fro across the rickety wooden bridge whenever they felt like it, eating the grass in the fields on both sides of the river. They were glad that they had stood up to the bullying troll.

Other people began to use the bridge to cross the river as well, and they would always stop and wave "Thank you" to the three Billy Goats Gruff.

"Don't tell me there's another goat coming behind you who's even bigger and fatter than you are!" the Troll said in surprise.

The eldest Billy Goat Gruff stood up straight and looked the troll straight in the eye. The troll really did look very fierce and very ugly, but the eldest Billy Goat Gruff was not going to let him see that he was frightened.

"There is no other goat coming after me. I am the last to cross the bridge," he said slowly and clearly.

"THEN I AM GOING TO GOBBLE YOU UP!" The troll's voice thundered out louder than ever.

"OH NO, YOU ARE NOT!" The voice of the eldest Billy Goat Gruff thundered out in reply.

All of a sudden, the eldest Billy Goat Gruff charged at the fierce ugly troll. With his head down, he butted the troll with his long curling horns as hard as he possibly could.

"BOOMPH!" The troll was tossed high into the air. "WHOOSH!" The troll flew right over the head of the eldest Billy Goat Gruff. "SPLASH!" The troll landed in the deep fast-flowing river and was swept right away downstream, never to be seen again.

The eldest Billy Goat Gruff tripped and trapped over the bridge to join his brothers in the big green field on the other side of the river.

The troll took a step towards the eldest Billy Goat Gruff. Down went the goat's head. "Thump, thump, thump!" went the front hooves of the eldest Billy Goat Gruff as he scraped them on the wood of the bridge in anger. The troll took another step towards the eldest Billy Goat Gruff. The goat's horns trembled with rage.

"THUMP, THUMP, THUMP!" his hooves pounded into the bridge more furiously. The troll hesitated a moment.

"THUMP, THUMP, THUMP!" The goat's hooves continued their pounding. The troll took another step towards the eldest Billy Goat Gruff.

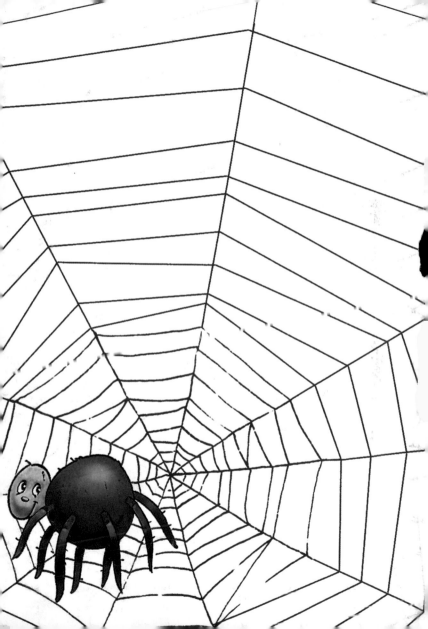